There's a monster in my house

Jenny Tyler and Philip Hawthorn

Illustrated by Stephen Cartwright

 There is a little yellow duck, a white mouse and a
spider on every double page. Can you find them?

There's a **monster** in my house

It's hungry, fierce and fat!

Don't be silly Milly

I think it's only...

There's a monster in my house

It's hiding in its den.

Don't be silly Milly

I think it's only...

There's a **monster** in my house

I'm scared to go in there!

Don't be silly Milly

I think it's only...

There's a **monster** in my shed

It's bound to eat my house!

Don't be silly Milly

I think it's only...